Young Learner's

Ginger's Special Birthday

HAPPY BIRTHDAY GINGER & BOBO

AF553121

ngita Koushik

© Young Learner Publications®, India

All rights reserved. No part of this publication may be reproduced, stored in a retrieval system, or transmitted in any form or by any means, electronic, mechanical, photocopying, recording or otherwise, without the prior written permission of Young Learner Publications, India.

Ginger was very excited. It was her birthday after all. As she got ready to go to school, she started thinking.

She thought of the lovely gifts she would get. And the yummy dishes her mother would prepare for the party.

She happily thought, "I will wear a very pretty dress for today's party." With this thought, Ginger went to school.

At school, everyone wished Ginger. She invited all her friends to her house for the birthday party in the evening.

Now, it was Ginger's classmate Bobo's birthday as well. Everyone wished her too. But Bobo did not look happy.

Ginger was surprised. She asked Bobo, "You look sad on your birthday. Why?" Tears rolled down Bobo's face.

She replied, "My parents will not host a party on my birthday. We do not have a lot of money."

Ginger felt bad for Bobo. She hugged Bobo. At home, Ginger thought about Bobo.

Suddenly, she had an idea, "Wow! Why did I not think of this before?" She told her parents her plan.

Later, the family decorated the room with balloons, birthday banner, pom poms, streamers, candles, etc.

The table was laid with yummy food like cupcakes, pastries, mini pizzas, brownies, tarts, burgers, juice, ice creams, and of course, the birthday cake!

Soon, the friends arrived with gifts. Ginger welcomed them to the party. She gave all of them party hats to wear and whistles to blow.

When everyone was there, Ginger said, "Friends, today we will be celebrating my birthday as well as Bobo's." She looked at Bobo.

She continued, "Bobo, please come here. Let us cut the cake together!" Bobo felt touched by Ginger's gesture. She gave her a tight hug.

Ginger and Bobo cut the cake together on which was written 'Happy Birthday Ginger and Bobo!' There were loud cheers! It turned out to be the best birthday after all. Ginger's parents were very proud of her.